Climb to the Sky

T0337095

Written by Rebecca Adlard

Illustrated by Amy Lane

Collins

What's in this story?

Listen and say

sheep

lion

chicken

Download the audio at www.collins.co.uk/839816

elephant

bear

rabbit

duck

Pip said, "What's this, Bo?"

Bo said, "It's Grandad Pete's hot air balloon, Pip."

Pip said, "A hot *bear* balloon?"

Bo said, "No! A hot *air* balloon."

Pip said, "What's a hot AIR balloon?"

Bo said, "It goes up in the sky. Grandad Pete says we can go up in his hot air balloon. Would you like to go up to the sky?"

Pip said, "Hmmmm ..."

Bo said, "Climb into the basket, Pip."

Pip said, "No, I don't think I want to go up in the sky, thank you."

Pip said, "I never go up in the sky, Bo."

Bo said, "Oh! Are you afraid?"

Pip said, "Oh no, I'm not afraid.
Well, I'm not *very* afraid."

Bo said, "Pip, do you know who first went in a hot air balloon?"

Pip said, "Was it a queen? A king?
An astronaut? Ooh, was it a film star?"

Bo said, "No, it was ...

... a chicken."

A long time ago in France, two brothers called Joseph and Étienne made a hot air balloon. They wanted to show the King their balloon. But they were afraid to get into the basket. So the chicken got in first.

Pip said, "Was the chicken afraid?"

Bo said, "Oh no!"

Pip climbed into the basket.
She said, "It's easy to get into the basket.
But I don't want to go up in the sky."

Bo said, "Oh Chicken does like it."

Pip said, "Does he?"

Bo said, "Yes, because he's got his friend Duck with him."

Pip said, "Duck?"

Pip said, "Were there any more animals in the balloon?"

Bo said, "Yes, there was one more.
Do you know what?"

Pip thought. Then she said, "Was it a ... rabbit? A lion?"

Bo and Pip said, "An elephant!"

That was funny.

"Oh, Pip! No! It was a ..."

Bo said, "Yes. A sheep. Its name was Montauciel."

Pip said, "That's a very interesting name."

Bo said, "It means climb to the sky. Montauciel the sheep went up in the sky."

Pip said, "Oh, it's easy to go up in the sky. But I don't think *I* want to go up in the sky."

The balloon went up and up into the sky.
Pip looked down. She saw the river below.
It was beautiful.

Pip says, "Wow! I love hot air balloons. So do Chicken, Duck and Sheep. It's easy to fly in a hot air balloon. I don't know why *you* were afraid, Bo!"

Picture dictionary

Listen and repeat

basket

hot air balloon

river

sky

down

up

1 Look and order the story

2 Listen and say

Collins

Published by Collins
An imprint of HarperCollins*Publishers*
Westerhill Road
Bishopbriggs
Glasgow
G64 2QT

HarperCollins*Publishers*
1st Floor, Watermarque Building
Ringsend Road
Dublin 4
Ireland

William Collins' dream of knowledge for all began with the publication of his first book in 1819.

A self-educated mill worker, he not only enriched millions of lives, but also founded a flourishing publishing house. Today, staying true to this spirit, Collins books are packed with inspiration, innovation and practical expertise. They place you at the centre of a world of possibility and give you exactly what you need to explore it.

© HarperCollins*Publishers* Limited 2020

10 9 8 7 6 5 4 3 2

ISBN 978-0-00-839816-3

Collins® and COBUILD® are registered trademarks of HarperCollins*Publishers* Limited

www.collins.co.uk/elt

British Library Cataloguing in Publication Data

A catalogue record for this publication is available from the British Library.

Author: Rebecca Adlard
Illustrator: Amy Lane (Beehive)
Series editor: Rebecca Adlard
Publishing manager: Lisa Todd
Product managers: Jennifer Hall and Caroline Green
In-house editor: Alma Puts Keren
Project manager: Emily Hooton
Editor: Rebecca Adlard and Frances Amrani
Proofreaders: Natalie Murray and Michael Lamb
Cover designer: Kevin Robbins
Typesetter: 2Hoots Publishing Services Ltd
Audio produced by id audio, London
Reading guide author: Matthew Hancock
Production controller: Rachel Weaver
Printed and bound by: GPS Group, Slovenia

MIX
Paper from
responsible sources
FSC™ C007454
www.fsc.org

Download the audio for this book and a reading guide for parents and teachers at www.collins.co.uk/839816